KEVIN HENKES
OLD BEAR

Greenwillow Books  *An Imprint of HarperCollinsPublishers*

For Virginia

Then he dreamed that it was summer.
The sun was a daisy, and the leaves were butterflies.

Part of the sky clouded over,
and it rained blueberries.

Next, he dreamed of autumn.

Everything was yellow and orange and brown,
even the birds and the fish and the water.